Tibby

PUBLISHED BY SCYTHE PUBLICATIONS, INC.
A Division of Winston-Derek Publishers Group, Inc.
Nashville, Tennessee 37205

Library of Congress Catalog Card No: 95-78544
ISBN: 1-55523-759-2

Printed in the United States of America

Tibby

DeeDee Reilly

DeeDee Reilly

Illustrations by
Betsy Walker

Betsy Walker

Scythe Publications, Inc.

A Division of Winston-Derek Publishers Group, Inc.

Hi, I'm a spruce tree. I lived on the side of a beautiful mountain until someone decided that I might be a very fine Christmas tree. So I was cut down and shipped to a town by the sea. That's where my story begins.

I was sitting on a large lot with many of my friends waiting for someone to buy me. I was worried about what would happen. Would anyone want me? Was I tall enough to be a Christmas tree? Too tall? Full enough? Too full? Would I be in a big house or a little house? In a church or in a store? Would the people be friendly? Would they be old or young? Would there be children?

Lots of people looked and walked on by. Maybe I wouldn't even be bought. Surely someone would want me. (They would have to.) Or at least I hoped so.

Then a lady with two dogs came my way, I put on my best smile and straightened my branches.

When I heard her saying nice things about me, I stood as tall as I could.

The owner of the lot came over and said to her, "Yes, Mrs. Doolie, that is a fine spruce tree." She told him that she wanted me.

A Christmas tree! I was going to be Mrs. Doolie's Christmas tree!

Spruce

for Sale

BW95

She took me to a wonderful house where there was beautiful music and sweet smells of baking. I was placed in front of a bright window where there were many plants and flowers and I knew I would have new friends. Then I was draped in colored lights and decorated with ornaments. I felt like a king and was truly happy.

One day I heard someone say that when Christmas was over, the trees were being put out on the street with other trash. Would that mean that my time was over? I tried not to think about it because it made me terribly sad and I was so happy with Mrs. Doolie.

When the holidays ended, Mrs. Doolie began removing my ornaments one by one and carefully placing them in boxes. As she put the last one away, she sighed and I knew my time had come. She lifted me from the stand and started toward the door. But you won't believe what she did!

Instead of taking me to the street, she took me out to the garden. There she poured honey on me and sprinkled bird seed on my branches. Soon the birds came to feed and sing to me. It was a perfect place to be!

One day, when a storm was
nearing, Mrs. Doolie took me to the beach
and laid me down near the water. She said I
could keep the sand from blowing away.

It was great fun out there with the hermit
crabs running under my branches and the
wind whistling about.

After the storm was over and the
wind had calmed, Mrs. Doolie
came and lifted me from the sand.
"Uh-oh," I thought to myself,
"I'm such a mess. Now I
am surely going to
the street."

But, instead, she took me to the back yard again and propped me in a corner. Before long a family of squirrels was swinging through my branches. We had lots of fun together.

Some months later I heard the gardener ask Mrs. Doolie if he should move me. She said, "Oh no, don't move Tibby!"

Tibby! Tibby! It was the first time she called me by a name. Tibby! I liked being Tibby. It was nice having a name. I decided that this must really be my home. She must really like me.

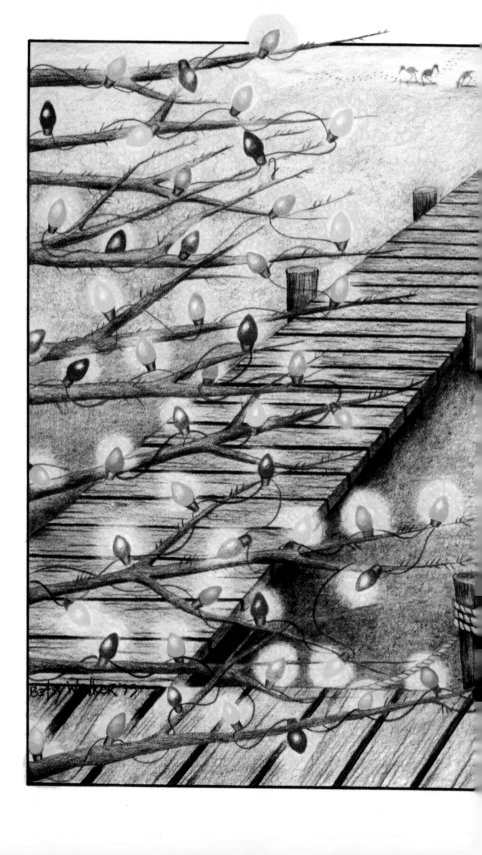

Fall arrived and the seasons changed again. When the holidays began, Mrs. Doolie took me to the end of her dock. She put lots of pretty colored lights on me so that people on boats out in the bay would be able to see a Christmas tree as they went by.

But before long, someone told Mrs. Doolie that I might be too dry to be covered in hot lights. They said I might catch on fire.

So once again, Mrs. Doolie took me to the garden and once again I didn't know what to expect. I did know though that it was time for her to pick out a tree for her house and some new tree would be taking my place. Well, much to my surprise, she began placing pinecones in my branches. That made me happy because pinecones are friends of mine. She kept puttting more and more pinecones on until I was full and round. There was just one problem. Each time Mrs. Doolie put a cone on one branch, another cone would fall out the other side. She tried wiring the cones to my branches, but we still had a problem. The cones on the inside were loose, and every time the wind blew, more cones dropped out.

Betsy Walker '76

Mrs. Doolie thought and thought about what to do. She finally decided to take me into the house. Behind us we left a trail of dropped pinecones and by the time we got inside I was nearly empty and quite bare. "Oh dear," I thought, "What is going to happen to me now?" But Mrs. Doolie seemed to have a plan.

She loaded the pinecones into a basket and brought them into the house.

She placed me in the exact spot by the big window where I had been the year before. It was then that I realized that it was me, Tibby, who was going to be the Christmas tree again!

Mrs. Doolie turned on the music and brought out more wire to secure the pinecones. Finally she added the strings of lights and beautiful ornaments. I was ready for another Christmas. I was so happy.

But the holidays were soon over and I was worried. What would happen to me now? Once again Mrs. Doolie looked like she had a plan. She stopped and thought, then she smiled as she boxed the Christmas ornaments and put them away.

"Oh dear, what next?" I thought.

Other boxes appeared and were opened. She took a beautiful garland of hearts and swirled it around my cones. Then she began to hang shiny wrapped candies. Finally she topped me with a big bright red valentine.

It was me, Tibby! I looked wonderful. I was a marvelous Valentine tree! Mrs. Doolie thought so, too.

So, this is the way I am still—full of love and happy. Sometimes I do wonder what will happen next.

For Easter, she wouldn't cover me with colored eggs would she?

What do you think?

The little spruce tree, Tibby, actually lives in Mrs. Reilly's garden. Tibby is now covered with beautiful purple-pink flowers called wisteria.

Trees can do so much more than hang Christmas lights and ornaments. They can celebrate other holidays, be homes for small animals, be a play toy for cats, act as a birdfeeder, be a friend for gardens, and much, much more.

How creative can you be with a tree?

About The Author

As a young mother driving carpools, Dee Dee Reilly began telling stories and found they kept children well occupied and always wanting more. Today she continues to entertain her grandchildren and young neighbors with her enchanting tales.

She and her husband are residents of Baton Rouge, LA, and spend time in Pensacola, FL, where this story evolved and Tibby has a place of honor in a special garden.

About The Illustrator

Betsy Walker lives in Pensacola, FL, with her husband and three young children. She is a graduate of Auburn University with a BFA in Illustration. This is her fifth collaboration on a children's picture book.